Zoo Party

by Ann M. Rossi
illustrated by Mick Reid

 HOUGHTON MIFFLIN   BOSTON

Printed in China

ISBN-13: 978-0-547-02642-8
ISBN-10: 0-547-02642-0

4 5 6 7 8 9 0940 15 14 13 12 11 10

Fox and Bear slept in caves inside their cages at the zoo. They came out of their caves every morning and said hello to the visitors.

Fox

The people loved to see
the animals.
And the animals loved to see
the people.

Bear

One day, Lion moved to the zoo.
Fox said, "Let's have a party so Lion
can meet all the animals!"
"That's a great idea!" said Bear.

Lion

Fox made a good plan for
the party.
She told her plan to Lion
and to the other animals.
They were all very excited!

Then Fox told the zookeeper
about the party.
"That's impossible,"
said the zookeeper.
"Animals don't have parties!"
The animals were very sad.
They went back into their caves.

Zookeeper

The visitors came to the zoo
the next day.
They wanted to see the animals.
But the animals did not come out
of their caves.
They did not say hello.
They were too sad.

Visitors

The people were very unhappy.
They went to talk to the zookeeper.
One boy said, "Where are
the animals?"
One woman said, "None of the
animals came to say hello!"

The zookeeper said to the visitors,
"I understand why you are upset.
I believe I can solve the problem,
and everyone will be happy.
Come back tomorrow."

That night, the animals had a
big party.
And the next day, they happily
came out of their caves.
The people loved seeing
the animals.
And the animals loved seeing
the people.
Now, the animals have a party
every time a new animal comes
to live at the zoo.

Party

Responding

Conclusions Why wouldn't the animals greet the visitors? Copy the chart. Add two details from the story that matches the conclusion.

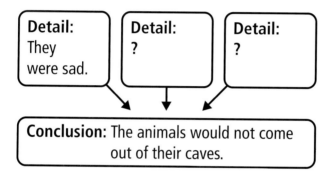

Detail:
They were sad.

Detail:
?

Detail:
?

Conclusion: The animals would not come out of their caves.

✏ Write About It

Text to Text Have you read a different story where a character asks someone to do something for them? Write a letter to persuade a character from a story to do something for someone else.

believe	impatient
demand	impossible
furious	problem
gathered	understand

✓ **TARGET SKILL** **Conclusions** Use details to figure out more about the text.

✓ **TARGET STRATEGY** **Infer/Predict** Use clues to figure out more about story parts.

GENRE **Humorous fiction** is a story that is written to make the reader laugh.